When I Was Little

A Four-Year-Old's Memoir of Her Youth

by Jamie Lee Curtis
illustrated by Laura Cornell

SCHOLASTIC INC.
New York Toronto London Auckland Sydney

The author wishes to thank Phyllis, Joanna, Marilyn, Laura, her family, and always, Chris

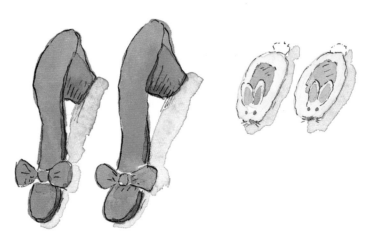

ISBN 0-590-03239-9

Text copyright © 1993 by Jamie Lee Curtis.
Illustrations copyright © 1993 by Laura Cornell.
All rights reserved. Published by Scholastic Inc., 555 Broadway, New York, NY 10012, by arrangement with HarperCollins Children's Books, a division of HarperCollins Publishers.

SCHOLASTIC and associated logos are trademarks and/or registered trademarks of Scholastic Inc.

12 11 10 9 8 7 6 5 4 3 2 1   8 9/9 0 1 2 3/0

Printed in the U.S.A.   08

First Scholastic printing, January 1998

For Annie
~J.L.C.

For Lilly
~L.C.

When I was little, I was a baby.

When I was little, I cried a lot.
Now I use words.

No

When I was little, I didn't know I was a girl.
My mom told me.

When I was little, I had silly hair. Now I can wear it in a ponytail or braids or pigtails or a pom-pom.

When I was little, I didn't get to eat Captain Crunch or paint my toenails bubble-gum pink.

When I was little, I spilled a lot.
My mom said I was a handful.
Now I'm helpful.

When I was little, I rode in a baby car seat. Now I ride like a grown-up and wave at policemen.

When I was little, I went to Mommy and Me.

Now I go to nursery school and I have teachers and cubbies and naptime and secrets.

When I was little, I didn't understand time-outs.
Now I do, but I don't like them.

When I was little, I made up words like "scoopeeloo."
Now I make up songs.

When I was little, I swam in the pool with boys. I still do, but now we wear bathing suits but we don't wear floaties.

When I was little, the slide at the park was so big.

Now it's smaller, but I still like my granny to wait at the bottom for me.

When I was little, I ate goo and yucky stuff.

Now I eat pizza and noodles and fruit and Chee-tos.

When I was little, I had two teeth.
Now I have lots, and I know how to brush
them.

When I was little, I slept in a zoo.
Now I sleep in a big bed and get to play
monkey.

When I was little, I kissed my mom and dad good night every night.
I still do, but only after they each read me a book and we play tickle torture.

When I was little, I didn't know what a family was.

When I was little, I didn't know what dreams were.

When I was little, I didn't know who I was.

Now I do!